# KEEPING MINIBE.

# SNAILS

## AND

# SLUGS

© 1988 Franklin Watts

First published in Great Britain in 1988 by
Franklin Watts
12a Golden Square
London W1

First published in the USA by
Franklin Watts Inc.
387 Park Avenue South
New York, NY. 10016

First Published in Australia by
Franklin Watts Australia
14 Mars Road, Lane Cove
New South Wales 2066

UK ISBN: 086313 691 5
US ISBN: 0-531-10621-7
Library of Congress Catalog
Card No: 88-50197

**Design:** Ben White
**Consultant:** C.H. Keeling

Printed in Italy by G. Canale & C. S.p.A. Turin

ISBN 0–531–15623–0 (pbk.)
First Paperback Edition 1991

# KEEPING MINIBEASTS

# SNAILS
## AND
# SLUGS

**TEXT: CHRIS HENWOOD**

**PHOTOGRAPHS: BARRIE WATTS**

## CONTENTS

FRANKLIN WATTS
LONDON • NEW YORK • SYDNEY • TORONTO

Snails and slugs are very similar to each other and in fact are quite closely related. Both are what is known as invertebrates. This means they have no backbones. They are also called mollusks.

The main way in which they differ from each other is that the snail has a shell.
It can withdraw into this in times of danger.

# Where they live

Snails and slugs can be found in similar areas of a garden or park. This is known as their habitat.

They like damp places, in between the stones of old walls, under damp stones and on the undersides of leaves.

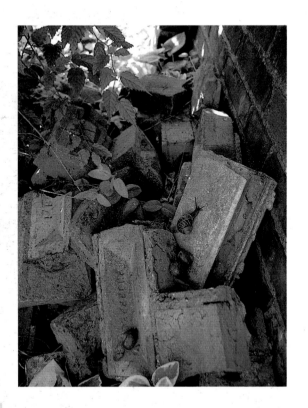

Both creatures are quite easy to find after the rain or in the early morning during the spring and summer.

# Collecting snails and slugs

Snails and slugs can be kept in almost any large wooden box or old fish tank. Even an old plastic sandwich box will do. If you use a lid, make sure it has holes in it.

The most interesting way to keep either pet is
in an old fish tank with a sheet of glass or
very fine mesh netting on a frame for a lid.

# Setting up a tank

Put 2 or 3 inches (5 or 8 cm) of gravel on the bottom of the tank. Make sure this is always kept moist.

Over this put a layer of damp soil and leaf litter and add a couple of large stones. Make sure that your soil has not been sprayed with chemicals.

Your stones should be arranged so that the snails can get underneath. Ideally, the soil and lower layers of the leaves should be moist and the upper layers dry.

# Feeding

Both snails and slugs will eat the same vegetable matter. This can be given to them in various ways like lettuce, apple or cucumber. You could also try other types of vegetables.

Just in case plants have been sprayed with chemicals, you should always wash the food before you feed any of it to your snails or slugs.

Remove any food that has not been eaten each day and replace it with fresh. Snails and slugs feed mainly at night so make sure that food is left for them in the evening.

Snails need calcium in addition to their food. This helps their shells to grow strong. The easiest way to provide this is to give them a piece of cuttlebone. One large piece from a pet store will last a few snails a long time.

# Breeding

If you keep your pets properly they should
live for a long time. Some may even lay eggs.
These are laid in hollows in the damp soil in
clusters of 20 to 40.

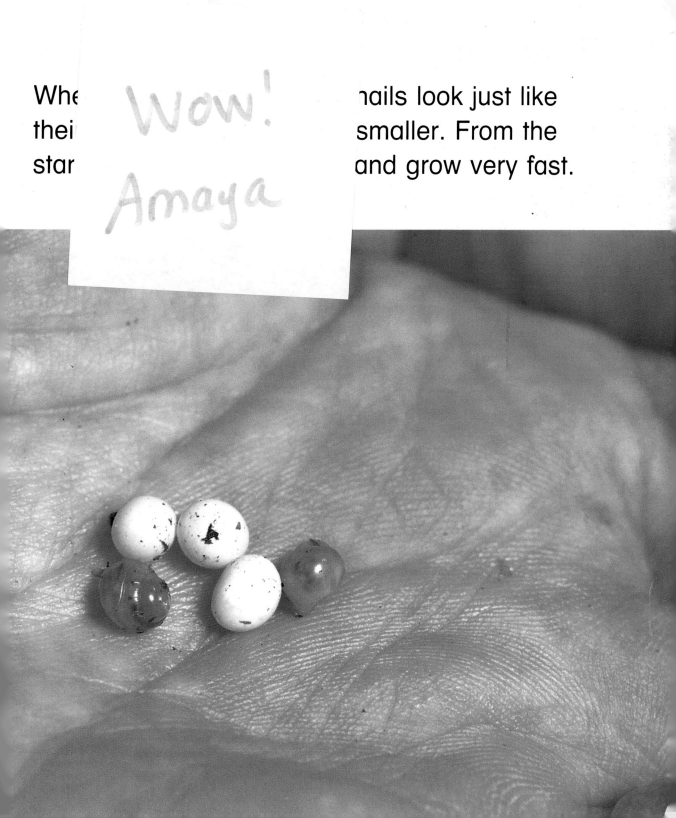

Whe[...] [s]nails look just like
thei[...] smaller. From the
star[...] and grow very fast.

*Wow!*
*Amaya*

# A closer look

Snails and slugs have soft bodies. On the snail you will see a breathing hole where the body joins the shell. In the slug this is usually found on the right side about half way along the body.

The eyes are on the end of long tentacles and look rather like little black pin heads. If you touch one gently the snail will pull it back for protection. Sometimes one eye will be pulled back while the other watches you.

If you put your snail or slug on a piece of glass you will be able to see its mouth. Watch it scrape at its food with its rough file-like tongue.

# Moving trails

Watch your snail or slug closely as it moves across the glass. You can see the muscles rippling along the body.

Both snails and slugs move along on a smooth layer of slime. It is this slime that causes the silvery trails you can often see. You can spot them on lawns and paths in gardens or streets.

# Hibernation

In winter both snails and slugs sleep, or hibernate, till spring. This happens because at this time of the year these animals find it very hard to find things to eat.

Snails find sheltered places under rocks, between logs and in cracks in walls. Here they stay, with a seal across their shell, until spring.

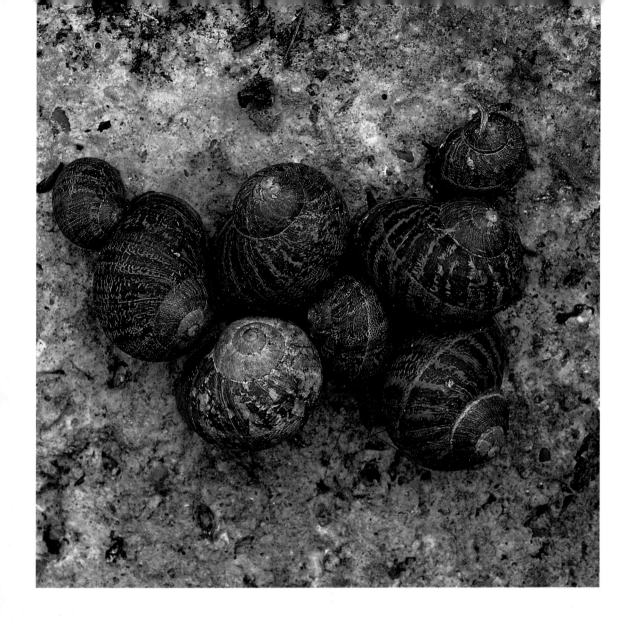

Because slugs do not have a shell to protect
them they burrow under stones or logs or just
into the soil for the winter.

When you go away you don't have to worry about finding someone to look after your pets for you. You can just let them go back to where you first caught them. Of course, you should only do this in summer **not** winter.

There are many types of snails. This Giant
African Land snail can be looked after in the
same way as its smaller relative.

# Unusual facts

Snails can lift ten times their own weight up a vertical surface. This is like a person lifting a ton.

The largest Giant African Land snail ever known weighed 2 lb (900 g) and measured 15.5 in (39.3 cm) from head to tail with a shell length of 10.75 in (27.3 cm).

Mr. Thomas Greene of La Plata, Maryland consumed 350 edible snails in just 8 minutes 29 seconds.

A special slime gland just behind the mouth of both snails and slugs releases a constant stream of slime over which the animal moves. When the surface of the ground becomes rougher the animal lays down more slime.

# Index